The Lord Is My Shepherd

By Hans Wilhelm

Little
Shepherd™
BOOKS

an imprint of

SCHOLASTIC

New York Toronto London Auckland Sydney
Mexico City New Delhi Hong Kong Buenos Aires

The Lord is my shepherd.

He gives me everything I need.

He lets me rest
in green pastures.

He leads me to quiet pools of water.
He gives me new strength when I am tired.

Because of His goodness,
He always leads me
along the right path.

Even in the darkest valley,
I am not afraid.
No evil can come to me.

Your shepherd's rod and staff make me feel safe.

You give me delicious food, even when there is danger around me.

You bless me.
I have more than
I could ever hold.

Your goodness and love will stay
with me all the days of my life.

And I will live in the house
of the Lord forever.